THE LOST LAMB AND THE FIND OF THE CENTURY

THE DISCOVERY OF THE DEAD SEA SCROLLS

J .Spencer Bloch

Illustrations by Hayim Roitblat Otsarya

ISBN: 978-965-7607-25-1

In the south of the Holy Land, the Negev Desert lies
It is hot and it's dry, as its name implies.
150 miles it stretches from the Red Sea
North through dunes and craters to the Dead Sea.

The Bedouin live there with camels, goats and sheep.

Each night in tents, on carpets, they sleep.

Each day these tribesmen take their flocks on the go.

There we start in 1947, a few miles from Jericho.

Muhammad "the Wolf," a young Bedouin man
Was trying to rescue his lost little lamb.
The lamb had wandered deep into a cave
In the hills of Qumran — could it be saved?

7

To scare the lamb out, he tossed in a rock.
What he then heard gave him quite the shock,
Not a thud, not a clatter, but a resounding crash
Like a vase hitting the floor, only to smash.

8

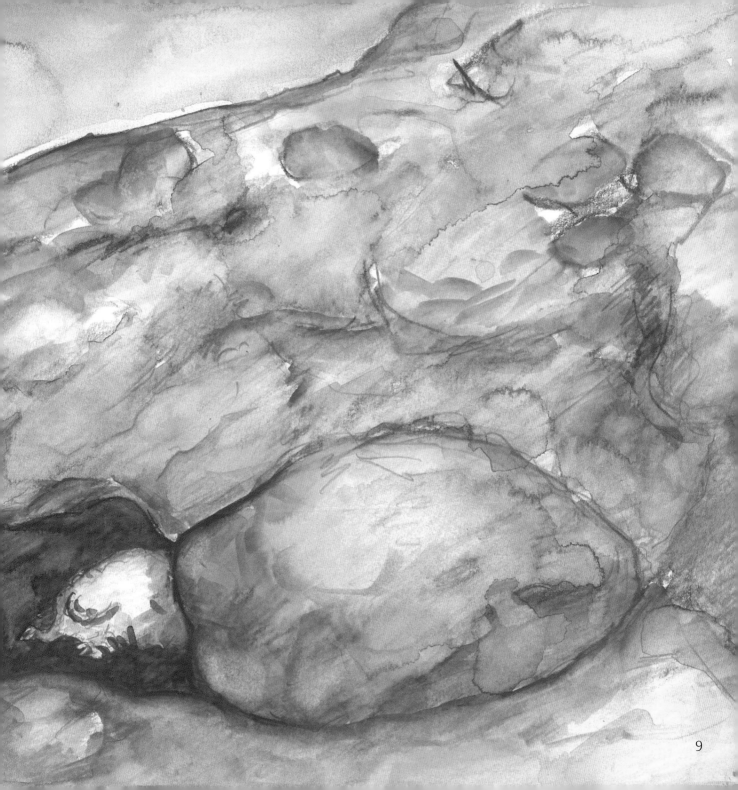

He hurried in to find ten jars made of clay

Most were empty, he discovered, to his dismay.

But ONE had some scrolls which seemed very old!

Muhammad puzzled over them, truth to be told.

The goatskin might be good for making some shoes,
So he took some scrolls home, with nothing to lose.
But his cousin stopped him as he picked up his blade –
They're ancient, he said, there's money to be made.

13

14

They were bought by a Syrian monk and a Jewish professor
Who realized that this shepherd had found a great treasure.
From far and wide, researchers came to Qumran.
To see eleven caves and a thousand scrolls from a time long gone.

These scrolls show the Holy Bible in its earliest form,
Studied by Jews in a community that was very warm.
They prayed in purity and kept baptismal rites,
Awaiting the Messiah and redemption through the dark nights.

16

Hayim O

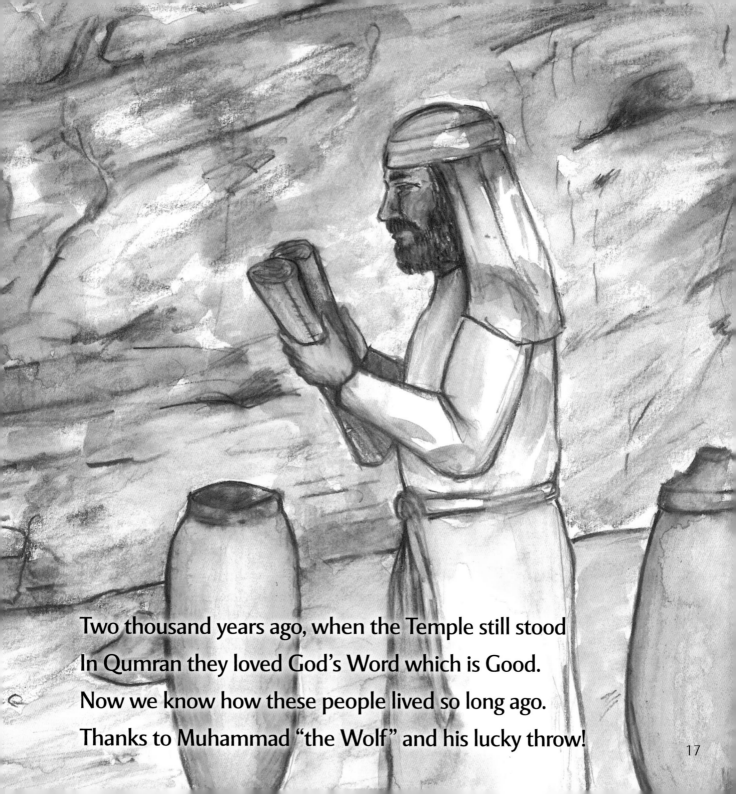

Two thousand years ago, when the Temple still stood
In Qumran they loved God's Word which is Good.
Now we know how these people lived so long ago.
Thanks to Muhammad "the Wolf" and his lucky throw!

17

The Dead Sea Scrolls are among the most important archeological discoveries in the Holy Land. These ancient manuscripts were initially found in the Judean Desert in the winter of 1946-1947 by a Bedouin shepherd. Ultimately, almost 1,000 different texts were found in eleven caves in the Qumran area over the next decade.

These manuscripts have immense scientific and theological value, as they contain the oldest remnants of the Bible in Hebrew. The community of scribes who created these texts is mysterious, but what is clear is that they date back to the last two centuries before the Common Era and depict a society eagerly awaiting the End of Days.

Over recent years, the scrolls have been digitized, allowing amateurs and scholars worldwide the opportunity to study them. The largest display is in the Shrine of the Book, part of the Israel Museum. Other fragments are in the Jordan Museum in Amman.

A number of the texts in the Dead Sea Scrolls contain enriching information about the lives of the members of the Judean Desert sect, who wrote these texts. It is noteworthy that the concepts of purification and penitence in the New Testament, as embodied in the character of John the Baptist, touch on this sect's worldview.

Jesus' social teachings also include concepts which echo this sect's worldview. Furthermore, the apocalyptic perspective which finds its roots in the Jewish Prophets and the descriptions in the New Testament (Armageddon) reaches its full expression in various writings of the sect, first and foremost in The War Scroll (also known as The War of the Sons of Light Against the Sons of Darkness).